The Nicky Fifth Series

Book 1
32 Dandelion Court
2007-2008 New Jersey Battle of the Books Selection

Book 2
Garden State Adventure
2005-2006 New Jersey Battle of the Books Selection

Book 3
For Hire

Nicky Fifth on

32 Dandelion Court

by Lisa Funari Willever

Franklin Mason Press
Trenton, New Jersey

For Jessica, Patrick, and Timothy, remember defeat is only
the inability to change your course...Mommy
To my husband, Todd, for everything.
To Rebecca & Dan Matthias, for your continued
interest and support.

Franklin Mason Press ISBN 978-0-9679227-7-5
Library of Congress Control Number 2003112515
10 9 8 7 6 5

Editorial Staff: Marcia Jacobs, Brooks Spencer, Linda Funari

www.franklinmasonpress.com

Contents

Chapter One

Four Leaf Clovers &
Mashed Potatoes

Some people have good luck, some people have bad luck, and then there is me. I never thought about luck, until I realized I had none. Once I wished for bad luck, because everyone knows that bad luck eventually turns good. If you have absolutely no luck, this never happens.

Six months ago, my life was normal; exactly how I liked it. I lived on Fifth Street in Philadelphia with my parents, my brother, and my two sisters. We lived in a two family house and my grandparents lived downstairs. I was the smallest kid in my fifth grade class, but it never mattered. I was the best pitcher in the little league and I knew what team I would play on until I turned 18 years old. I had a routine and more importantly, I liked my routine. Everything was good.

Then came St. Patrick's Day. I thought I knew exactly how my day would go. Our house would be decorated with wall-to-wall clovers and dinner would be green. My mom taught kindergarten and every activity she did at school, she did at home. At 6:00, my father would come home, see the clover-covered house, and shake his head. At 6:15 we would sit down to dinner. After our Key Lime pie, I would finish my homework, play some games, watch television, and go to sleep.

But this year was different. When my

father came home from work, he was smiling and walked right past the clovers without shaking his head. He went straight to the kitchen, picked up my mother, and gave her a big kiss. I should have known that this meant trouble.

My dad was a produce manager at the Fresh Market grocery store and he never met a fruit or vegetable he didn't like. He grew up in South Philadelphia and, like me, he had a routine that he liked. I couldn't imagine what his big news would be, but I was sure it was harmless. Maybe he discovered a new variety of apple.

"What's up?" asked my mom.

"I have news that will change the rest of our lives."

I remember thinking that his was too big to be a new apple, it must have been a new type of lettuce. While my mom added green food coloring to the mashed potatoes, my dad paced the kitchen floor. I felt like a spectator at a tennis match. I tried to catch his eye, thinking he might tell me his news first. After five minutes and a sore neck, I still knew nothing.

My brother, Timmy, walked into the kitchen first. He was nine years old and did everything I did. He was worse than a shadow. At least you can lose a shadow in the dark. Timmy was never more than two steps behind me, day and night.

Two minutes later, Maggie strolled in with her usual companions, three rag dolls that, as my grandmother says, have seen better days. It was easy to know where Maggie was in the house. She talked to imaginary friends and she had peanut-butter breath. She was four years old and more fun to watch than to play with.

My mom returned carrying Emma, my two year old sister. While it was funny to watch Maggie talk *to herself*, it was funnier to talk *to Emma*. By the time she was speaking in sentences, I had found a new hobby - teaching her new words to songs and nursery rhymes. As my mom strapped her into her high chair, she started to sing my latest creation.

"Wo, wo, wo your goat, gently down the stream. Merrily, merrily, merrily...hey, who the heck is Merrily? Life is butter cream!"

My mom raised one eyebrow and looked at me. She obviously didn't appreciate my creativity, even though she's the one that encourages me to use my imagination. There's just no pleasing some people.

We sat at the table watching my mom bring in our dinner. One dish was greener than the next. We had green ham, green mashed potatoes, green buttered noodles, and green peas. She poured everyone a glass of green lemonade and held up her glass. It was time for her St. Patrick's Day toast. We raised our glasses and sippy cups.

"May the road rise up to meet you. May the wind always be at your back. May the sun shine warm upon your face and rains fall softly on your fields. Cheers!"

And with that, the official St. Patrick's Day dinner began. Except for my mom, I doubt any of us understood what she said, but it seemed to make her happy. She began filling our plates and, for a moment, forgot all about my father's big news.

"Well," he began. "I have some big news for the Abruzzi Family. Anyone interested?"

"Oh, that's right kids. Your father has a surprise for us. Go ahead, honey."

Except for the sounds of my mom's Irish CD playing 'When Irish Eyes Are Smiling', the kitchen became very quiet.

"You know how we've always talked about moving out of the city? Well, I found a great house in the country with a big yard. I left work yesterday and went to see it. The owners are moving to California, so I made an offer!"

Suddenly, no Irish eyes were smiling. Everyone just stared at my dad. For the first time in my life, my mom was speechless. This was a first.

"I know this is probably a shock," he continued, "but I just know you'll fall in love with the house and the neighborhood when you see it!"

It was too early to be an April Fools joke, but I was still waiting for the punch line. Silence. No one moved or spoke a word. We looked like a display from the wax museum. Then, my mom asked the question we all wanted to ask.

"Are you serious?"

"Sure, I'm serious. Think about it. We always talked about raising the kids in the country and now it can happen!"

"We're moving to another country?" Timmy asked.

"Not another country," my dad laughed. "To the country, out of the city, where there's room to play."

I finally found the words I was looking for and before I could stop them, they all started coming out. "You mean you want us to move to another neighborhood so we'll have more room to play? That's ridiculous. We have plenty of room right here. And what about my friends? How far will I have to ride my bike to hang out with my friends?"

"Nick," my dad said, looking me in the eye, "there are no country houses in the city. We'd be leaving Philadelphia."

"Leaving Philadelphia?" I yelled.

"Nick, we'd be moving to New

Jersey."

"New Jersey?" I asked in a panic. "My friends aren't allowed to ride their bikes over the Ben Franklin Bridge. How will I see my friends?"

As the tension grew, I noticed my mom from out of the corner of my eye. I realized that she hadn't said anything yet. While everyone had at least blinked by now, mom looked like one of the ice sculptures at cousin Rosalie's wedding. It only took a few seconds before my father noticed this, too.

"Honey, you haven't said anything yet. What do you think?"

"You made an offer without asking me?"

Now he did it. I suddenly felt a sigh of relief shoot through my body. There was no way we would move now. If there was one thing my mom hated, it was when my dad made a decision without asking her. The last time he made a decision without her was when he came home with golf wallpaper. Just like she made him return the wallpaper, she would make him return the house. This was a huge mistake and I could think of no way for him to get out of this one. Hopefully, he had the receipt.

"Erin, I told the owners that my offer would be contingent upon your approval. I wasn't trying to exclude you, honey, I just wanted to give you the surprise of your life."

Whoa! He did it. He got around the *We Make Decisions Together* rule by using the *Surprise of Your Life trick*. Surely, my mom was too clever to fall for that line.

"Alright, give me a second here," she said, rubbing her forehead. "This is definitely the biggest shock of my life."

"I'll tell you what," my dad said, "after dinner we'll take a ride to the house and you can check it out yourself."

"As long as we're not locked into buying this house, it wouldn't hurt to take a look at it. But I'm not making any promises," said my mom.

And that was that.

can check it out, right?"

"...as well not buy them now, impulse house, it wouldn't hurt to take a look..."

Chapter Two

32 Dandelion Court

The rest of our dinner was pretty quiet, except for Maggie who continued to talk to her dolls and a few friends only she could see.

I tried to enjoy the rest of my meal but it all tasted the same. I'm not sure if it was because everything on my plate was green or that the world, as I knew it, was coming to an end.

One thing was certain, my father was excited. We knew this when he started to clear the dishes and load the dishwasher. For a man that was never formally introduced to our appliances, this was an event. My mom carefully monitored his every move and when he finished, he actually bowed. We weren't sure if we should clap or call a doctor. Unable to decide, we continued to stare.

"I'll go get changed," my father announced, closing the door to the dishwasher. "You're all set, Erin. You can start her up."

Without knowing it, my father confirmed something we had always suspected. He did not know how to turn on the dishwasher. As my mom opened it up and began reloading, she realized one more thing. He did not know how to load a dishwasher.

"Nicky, grab Emma's shoes for me," said my mom.

With my dad out of the room, those were the only words spoken. I couldn't speak for anyone else, but there were too many things running through my mind to talk. I didn't know where to begin. I could not imagine leaving Philadelphia, let alone moving to New Jersey.

My whole identity was linked to my neighborhood. All of my friends called me Nicky Fifth because I lived on Fifth Street. I wondered what the chances of my dad moving us to another Fifth Street were. I figured they weren't too good.

The drive to the Ben Franklin Bridge seemed much longer than it actually was. Thirty minutes later, we arrived. The first thing I noticed was the names of the streets. As we drove through, each name was worse than the next. We turned onto Hibiscus Lane, made a right on Lily of the Valley, and passed Petunia Road, Jasmine Way, and Dandelion Court. Suddenly, my dad slowed down and I realized the unthinkable, our new house might be on Dandelion Court, 32 Dandelion Court, to be precise.

A million things went through my mind, but first and foremost was the fact that I would never be called Nicky Fifth again, I'd now be known as Nicky Dandelion.

We parked in the driveway and I carefully scanned the street. The houses were nice enough, had big yards, and I could see dozens of swing sets and pools in most of the yards. There was only one problem besides the name of the street. The house and neighborhood were in New Jersey and I had no intention of leaving Philadelphia.

My dad turned off the car, got out, and started walking to the house. He made it halfway there when he realized that we were all still in the car.

"I guess we should join him," my mom sighed.

It was clear that she did not want to

move. She was going through the motions, but her heart definitely wasn't in it. Mom was my only hope, the only thing keeping me in Philadelphia and on Fifth Street. I decided to feel her out.

"Mom, we're not really going to move to New Jersey, are we?" I asked with the saddest face I could manage.

"Don't worry Nicky," she said as she unfastened the girls from their seatbelts. I'm sure this is just a phase. It's not the first time he's found the perfect house."

"Really?" I asked.

"Yes, just act like you're okay with it and I guarantee he'll change his own mind." At this point, I wasn't sure if she was trying to convince me or herself.

"Are you sure we're really not going to move?"

"Honey, I have no intentions of moving. I've learned to just smile, be polite, and wait until the mood passes. Relax and follow my lead."

Famous last words, I thought.

My dad rang the doorbell and seconds later a man opened the door.

"Jim, good to see you," he said as they shook hands.

"Erin, this is Don Woodward. Don, this is my wife, Erin and our four children."

My mom fake-smiled and shook his hand.

"Please, come in," Mr. Woodward said.

We walked in and I checked the house for any reason it wouldn't be right for us. Within seconds, I realized that this would be harder than I thought. The living room was twice as big as our living room, they had a dining room, a downstairs bathroom, and a garage. If this were a poker game, we would have already lost.

As we continued on the tour of doom, I caught a glimpse of my mom's face. She looked like my dad at a roadside fruit stand. I realized that the only thing standing between me and New Jersey was the kitchen. My mom loved to bake and always wished she had a great big kitchen. If this house had a big kitchen, there was no chance we would stay in Philadelphia.

Just when I thought things couldn't be worse, I noticed a familiar smell. My heart stopped. It was chocolate chip cookies, my mom's downfall.

Oh no, I thought.

I followed the crowd into the kitchen and there it was, the biggest, newest kitchen I had ever seen. I didn't need to look at my mom's face to know she was grinning from ear to ear and it wasn't a fake smile.

"Hello, everyone," said the woman,

carefully placing the cookies on a dish.

"Jim and Erin, this is my wife, Barbara," said Mr. Woodward.

"It's nice to meet all of you. You have such beautiful children," she said with a smile. "Please, help yourself to some cookies."

Maybe my mom hated the kitchen. Maybe she knew that a bigger kitchen would mean bigger messes. Before I could finish hoping, I heard my mom speak to Mrs. Woodward."Your kitchen is amazing. I've always wanted a kitchen like this!"

"Me, too!" said Mrs. Woodward. "We just had the house remodeled last spring. This move to California came up very suddenly."

"Well, you did a lovely job," my mom gasped as she opened the double oven.

Great, two ovens. What was next?

"Where does this door lead?" my mom

asked.

"Oh, that's the walk-in pantry."

I knew I was in trouble when my mom didn't come right out. After a couple of minutes, I peeked inside to see what was going on. "Look at the size of this pantry, Nick!" she whispered. "Can you believe this kitchen?"

"Would you like to see the upstairs?" Mr. Woodward asked.

There's more, I thought.

"Sure," my parents giggled.

Things didn't get better when we reached the top step. There were four bedrooms, two bathrooms, and a linen closet. As we entered the master bedroom, I knew it was all over. The room was enormous and the master bathroom was as big as my bedroom at home.

"Wow," said my mom, covering her mouth with her hand.

"Show them the fireplace, dear," said Mrs. Woodward.

Fireplace? Fireplace?

With a flick of the switch a fire started in the fireplace. After this, the rest of the tour is a blur. As everyone went outside to see the deck, I went out front and sat on the steps. No one noticed. Thirty minutes later, I was still sitting on the steps, alone.

My parents were so in love with this house, they didn't even notice I was gone. Moments later, everyone was exchanging goodbyes and promising to have their real estate agents contact each other.

We piled into the van and headed back to Philadelphia. I stared out the window but don't remember much of what I saw.

"Well, kids, what do you think? Don't you just love it?" asked my dad.

"I wove it," Emma giggled.

Traitor, I thought.

"Can my dolls move with me?" asked Maggie.

"Of course they can," my mom laughed.

"Where are the cows?" Timmy wondered out loud.

"Timmy, it's in the country, but it's not a farm!"

"You're awful quiet, Nick," my dad finally noticed.

I had to come up with a good reason why we shouldn't buy this house. Unfortunately, I was a drawing a blank.

Chapter Three

Around The Block

The next day I felt horrible. I tried to imagine what New Jersey kids were like. I didn't know if they watched the same shows, liked the same music, or if they played baseball. I only knew one thing, they weren't my friends. My dad always joked and called my friends a bunch of knuckleheads, but they were my knuckleheads.

These were my best friends and they each had a nickname. I was called Nicky Fifth, because I lived on Fifth Street. Whenever I pitched, everyone on the bench and in the stands would yell, "Fifth, Fifth!"

Joey Carlucci was called Joey Grapes, because he was such a sore loser. His tee ball coach always called him Joey Sour Grapes, but eventually it was shortened. He outgrew tee ball years ago, but we doubted he'd ever outgrow his temper.

Benny Bones was really skinny and you could count his ribs when he didn't wear a shirt. Most people would be embarrassed, but not Benny. Whenever it got slightly warm, Benny took off his shirt and told people to count his ribs.

Gino Pie never left home without a piece of cake or pie in his hand. He should have weighed 300 pounds, but he was pretty tall and thin. We figured it was because as he finished one pie, he ran for the next one.

Bobby Boots wore red rain boots everyday, rain or shine, until third grade. His mother always carried a pair of sneakers in the car, hoping that one day he would take off the boots. On the first day of third grade, he wore sneakers and we hardly recognized him.

Crazy John lived in the neighborhood his whole life and the craziest thing he ever did was swallow his gum, and even that was an accident. He was probably the most trustworthy, dependable guy in the group and if we hadn't known him all of our lives, we never would have hung out with him. My mom liked to think he was a good influence on us, but my father swore he had to have a dark side. Ironically, they were both wrong.

Then there was Freddie Dragon, except no one ever called him Dragon. His real name was Freddie Kohler and he wanted a nickname so bad, he made one up himself. By making up his own nickname, he broke Nickname Cardinal Rule Number 1: *you can never give yourself a nickname.* We almost felt bad for him. No matter how hard he tried, the name would not stick. His mother wouldn't even call him Dragon and he tried to pay her.

I looked around the lunch table. Everyone was talking and laughing and having a good time, I couldn't tell them I was moving. I couldn't say it out loud. I started hoping the Woodward's would stay in New Jersey. I wondered why anyone who had a chance to move out of New Jersey would want to stay.

I didn't know if they would think moving to New Jersey was really lame or really cool. I wished I knew what they would say. Finally, I decided to make up a story about a friend who was moving to New Jersey. It was the perfect way to see what they thought about New Jersey.

"Hey, did you guys hear that Mikey Jones is moving to Jersey?"

"Who's Mikey Jones?" asked Joey Grapes.

"You know, the tall kid that lives around the block," I said.

There really was no Mikey Jones, I just wanted to see their reaction. I threw out the bait and hoped they would bite.

"I never heard of a Mikey Jones," added Benny Bones.

"Yeah, you've seen him before. He's real tall and quiet," I said.

"What street does he live on? I thought I knew everyone," Joey Grapes persisted.

I couldn't believe it. Rather than talk about New Jersey, they were ready to send out a search party for my imaginary friend.

"Forget it," I said kind of aggravated. "I just thought you knew him."

"Wait a minute," said Freddie. "I know him. I didn't know he was moving."

Leave it to Freddie to lie about knowing someone I just invented. The worst part was, to prove he was lying, I would have to admit that I made up Mikey Jones. I decided to drop it, when Boots suddenly spoke up.

"That's a shame," he said. "I would hate to move to New Jersey. They only have two roads, the Turnip and the Parkway. They don't even have towns, they just have exit numbers."

"They have towns," said Benny Bones, "but you have to pay when you drive on the roads."

"All the roads?" asked Freddie.

"I think so," said Joey Grapes.

"Do you have to pay to drive down your street?" Gino Pie wondered.

"No," I said, becoming very impatient. "I don't think you have to pay to drive on all of the roads. And it's the Turnpike, not the Turnip."

"Still, I'd hate to move there," said

Bobby Boots. "My dad says that you aren't even allowed to pump your own gas."

Great, I thought. I didn't find out how they felt about New Jersey, the only thing I learned is that my friends don't get out much. Luckily, driving to New Jersey the night before, I knew most of what they were saying was wrong.

Joey Grapes thought for a moment then continued. "My uncle Louie lives in Jersey and he says that so many people live there, they've built houses on all of the farmland. The worst part is that they ran out of normal street names. My uncle lives on Pumpkin Drive and his boss lives on Tea Party Lane."

"No wonder they don't have a baseball team," added Gino Pie. "What major leaguer would want to live on Tea Party Lane?"

Perfect. How could I tell my friends that I was moving to Dandelion Court?

Maybe I wouldn't have to tell them. If they asked for my address, I could give them a fake one. Maybe I could find some nice person who lives on a cool street and they could forward my mail. Maybe I could rent a post office box. I wondered if they rented them to kids.

I decided my secret could wait.

Chapter Four

A Wise Old Man Once Said

I couldn't help wondering how could this be happening to me? Little League would start in April and I would have been the starting pitcher, again. I even had my eye on the Little League World Series. Didn't my father realize that I was in my prime? Playing on a new team would definitely screw up my momentum.

Then, I had the most horrible thought. Did they even have Little League in New Jersey? Maybe they have no professional baseball team because all the kids spend their summers collecting tolls or pumping gas. Maybe they had no room for baseball fields, because too many people lived there.

On the way home from school, I decided it was time to go over my mom's head. I went downstairs, to my grandparents' house, and looked for my grandfather. He was one of my best friends and I was sure that he would order my mom and dad to stay in Philadelphia. I went downstairs and knocked on the door.

"Come in, Nicky," Pop yelled.

"How did you know it was me?"

"I talked to your mom this morning. I've been expecting you."

"So you know? You know that they want to move us to New Jersey?"

"I know all about it," he said.

"Well, I hope you put your foot down and ordered them to stay."

My grandfather smiled. "Listen Sport, I can't make your parents stay. They're adults with their own family and they have every right to decide where they will live."

"Are you kidding? That's it? You're not even going to try reverse psychology? There has to be something we can do. I can't move to New Jersey."

"Nicky, your parents have talked about moving out of the city since you were a baby. Every time they came close, something happened, usually a new baby. But it sounds like they found a nice house in a nice neighborhood. You just have to give it a chance."

"Pop, you don't understand. Did they tell you the name of the street they want us to move to?"

"No, I don't recall them saying the name of the street. Why?"

"They want us to move to 32 Dandelion Court! Dandelion Court! I'm Nicky

Fifth, not Nicky Dandelion."

My grandfather started to laugh, again.

"It's not funny," I pleaded. "How would you like to grow up on Dandelion Court?"

"I'm not laughing at you," he said, still laughing. Then, he went into his bedroom and came out with a picture in his hand. "Take a look at this."

I looked at the old, tattered black and white picture of a little boy in a suit with short pants and a feather in his hat.

"Who's the dork?" I asked.

"For your information, that dork is me. Now turn it over, wiseguy."

I turned it over and read the back.

Timothy Abruzzi

Age 6

Ladybug Lane, Newtown, PA

"You lived on Ladybug Lane?" I asked.

"Some of the best days of my life were spent on Ladybug Lane. We had a country house, with a front porch swing and plenty of room to run and play."

"But I thought you always lived in the city."

"No, I was raised in the country. Your grandmother and I moved into the city when we got married. Every Sunday we brought your dad and your aunts and uncles to see their grandparents in the country. Your dad always said he wanted to live there one day."

"But why now? If he's been saying 'one day' for years, why can't he wait until I leave for college? And what about my friends and you and Grandmom?"

"Kiddo, you'll always have your friends and you'll make new ones, too. It's not like the days of the Pony Express. You can talk on the phone, e-mail each other, and you'll see them when you come visit us."

Visit, I thought. In all of my life, I never visited my grandparents. I visited a lot of other relatives, but never Gram and Pop. We just went downstairs and barged in whenever we wanted. I wondered if we would have to knock.

"But you and Grandmom have always lived downstairs. How do I get used to that? Where do I go when there's a line for the bathroom?"

"From what I've heard about your new house, there's plenty of bathrooms."

"But we hang out everyday. You're okay with only seeing me on the holidays?"

"You're not moving to the moon," my grandfather laughed. "You're moving over the bridge and down the road. And sure we're going to miss seeing you guys everyday, but we never thought you'd live here forever. Plus, I think you guys will be here often!"

"You don't understand," I mumbled.

"Try to get some sleep and we'll talk tomorrow. Put yourself in your father's shoes and you may see things differently."

Suddenly, I had a brilliant idea. At least I thought it was brilliant. "What if I move in with you and Grandmom? I could do things around the house. I could even cook and clean. It'll be great."

Before I could answer, my grandmother walked in the family room, laughing.
"We've seen how you cook and clean, Nick. I don't think so," she said, winking at my grandfather.

"Then why don't you guys move to New Jersey? If it's as great as you say it is, I'm sure we could find you a house on our great new street."

"We're a little too old to start all over again, sport," my grandfather said.

We just sat there in silence. Back to the drawing board. I tried to think of another solution and then it came to me.

"Maybe Joey Grapes can talk his family into moving to New Jersey. Maybe all of the guys could move, too. It wouldn't be so bad if I brought everyone with me. It would be just like Philadelphia."

"Nick, when you move to New Jersey, you can't bring Philadelphia with you. You never move your igloo south."

And there it was. I knew it wouldn't be long before he came out with one of those expressions that I never understood. I was sure he said these things to confuse me, especially since I don't have an igloo.

"Whatever," I mumbled.

Chapter Five

Walk A Mile In His Shoes

I didn't find my grandfather's advice all that helpful. I went to bed, but that's all I did. I didn't sleep. I just tossed and turned. I tried to think about the situation from my father's point of view, and I decided that I didn't care about his feelings. After all, he certainly wasn't thinking about my feelings.

Around two o'clock in the morning, I saw my bedroom door open and four heads appeared. I rubbed my eyes and took another look. It was Maggie and an armful of dolls.

"Nicky, are you in here?"

"Yeah, what do you want?" I asked. I was expecting her usual nonsense.

"I don't not want to leave my house and I don't not want to leave Grandmom."

For the first time in her life, she was making sense. It was at this moment, I realized I just may have an ally, actually four allies if I counted the dolls. Maybe she could convince my parents to stay.

"Did you tell mommy that you don't want to leave?" I asked.

"No, I told Sarah to tell her."

Great, I thought. Sarah was a rag doll.

"Maybe you should tell her," I suggested.

"Why don't you tell Grandpop?" she asked.

"I did talk to Grandpop tonight. He said I have to put myself in Dad's shoes and go to sleep."

"Why?" she asked.

"It's complicated. Why don't you and your friends go back to your room before mommy hears you."

I wanted her to leave before she woke up Timmy. Not being able to sleep was bad enough, but having my shadow watch me toss and turn would have been worse.

A moment later she was gone and I was still awake. I kept thinking about how great my life was before St. Patrick's Day. Now, just two days later, everything was out of control.

I knew my dad loved going to the country on Sundays, everyone knew that. We were the only family in the neighborhood that went on Sunday rides. Week after week, no matter how much I begged or pleaded, I had to go. We would drive around for hours and stop at farms and farm markets. My father would admire the fruits and vegetables and then make us 'moo' at the cows.

This may have been the only bright spot to moving to the country. Maybe we would stop driving to the country if we already lived there.

When the alarm went off, I felt like I had just closed my eyes. I hit the snooze button and rolled over. I was dreaming about the Little League Championship game and I wanted to try to finish the dream. Before I could try, I heard my mom shriek.

I ran down the hall to my parents' room. I couldn't believe my eyes. My mom found Maggie and her dolls, sleeping in her closet. She was laying on her back and wearing a pair of my dad's black dress shoes. Worse yet, she had each doll standing in a pair of my dad's shoes.

"Maggie, wake-up," my mom said as she nudged her. "What on earth are you all doing in our closet?"

As she asked the question, I remembered what I had said the night before. Before I could run back to my room, I heard Maggie's response. "Nicky told me to wear dad's shoes."

"What?" my dad said, glaring at me. "What did you tell her to do that for?"

Before I could answer, Maggie did a little more damage.

"Nicky told us to wear your shoes and go to sleep. I couldn't not carry them and these dolls, so I slepted here cause I'm smart."

My mom looked at me with her raised eyebrow.

"You know how she is," I started to defend myself. "It's like when you told her to eat all of her vegetables because there were people starving in our own backyard and she left sandwiches out back for a week."

After I reminded them of Maggie's work to help the hungry, no one hollered at me. I wasn't officially cleared, but the subject was quickly dropped. My mom scooped up Maggie and her crew and brought them back to the girls' bedroom.

For a brief moment I felt like an adult. I looked at my dad and he looked at me.

"Kids," I said, as I rolled my eyes.

He closed the door on me.

Chapter Six

The Shadow Speaks

By the time I got to school, I could hardly keep my eyes open. All of the tossing and turning was catching up with me. I was yawning so much that one yawn started before the first one was finished.

On top of that, all of my friends were still talking about Mikey Jones. I wondered if they would miss me as much they were going to miss my made-up friend. Gino even talked about throwing Mikey a going away party. Of course, Gino looked for any excuse to have his mom bake more pies.

As the day wore on, I felt like I could fall asleep right at my desk and that's just what I did. The last thing I remembered about math class was Mrs. Bailey telling us to take out our homework. Apparently, I slept through the whole class and two bells. Two hours had gone by before I woke up. When I did wake up, I didn't recognize any-one sitting next to me. As I rubbed my eyes, I saw Mrs. Bailey heading toward my desk.

"Good morning," she said.

"Huh?" I asked, very confused.

"I hope we didn't disturb you, Nicholas."

I tried to sit up straight and act natural, but it clearly wasn't working. I glanced at the girl next to me and noticed she had an Eng-lish book on her desk. Then I saw Joey Grapes and I knew something was wrong.

Joey wasn't in my math class!

What time was it? Before my humiliation could continue, the final bell rang. Mrs. Bailey excused everyone except me.

"Nicholas, can I see you at my desk? Everyone else, have a good day and don't forget your book reports are due tomorrow."

I slowly walked up to her desk. "What happened?" I asked.

"Funny, that's what I was going to ask you," Mrs. Bailey said. Just like my mom, she raised one eyebrow when she spoke. I figured it was a teacher thing.

"I guess I was tired," I mumbled.

"Pretty safe guess," she said without looking up. "Have a seat, Nick."

"Yes, Mrs. Bailey."

"Now, this type of behavior isn't like you. So, we can play twenty questions or you can just tell me what's going on."

If I was going to fall asleep in anyone's

class, I was kind of glad it was with Mrs. Bailey. She was one of the younger teachers, but she was no pushover. She was very strict, but also funny. I was hoping she still had her sense of humor.

"I didn't get too much sleep last night."

"Are you sick?" she asked.

"No."

"Okay," she said, looking me right in the eye. "Why didn't you sleep? Are you worried about the mortgage? Is your car in the shop? Are your kids giving you a hard time?"

"No," I said, trying not to smile. "I just found out that we're moving."

"Oh," she said. "Where are you moving?"

I couldn't say the words. If I said it out loud, it would have made it true. So I stared at my shoe, pretending I didn't hear the question. Mrs. Bailey didn't buy it.

"Let's see," she said as she spun the globe on her desk. "Paris?"

"No."

"Greece?"

"No."

"Kansas?"

"No," I said with a smirk. "New Jersey. My parents are dragging us over the Ben Franklin Bridge to New Jersey."

"And I guess you're not happy about this?"

"Happy?" I asked. "Who in their right mind would be happy about moving to New Jersey? I don't even think the people that live in New Jersey are too happy about it. They just don't know any better."

"Arc you more mad that you're leaving Philadelphia or that you're going to New Jersey?"

"Both," I said.

"You know, New Jersey isn't that different from Pennsylvania," she said matter-of-factly.

"But it's not Philadelphia," I insisted.

"But you might like it."

"I doubt that anyone likes living in New Jersey."

"Really," Mrs. Bailey said, looking over her glasses. Then she opened her purse and pulled out her wallet.

Maybe she's giving me money to run away, I thought.

She pulled out her license, keeping her thumb over the picture, and placed it in front of me.

I looked twice and I still couldn't believe it. Mrs. Bailey lived in New Jersey! She never mentioned that to us, I would have remembered.

"You live in New Jersey?" I asked.

"Ever since I married Mr. Bailey,"

"But you love the Phillies, the Flyers,

the Sixers, and the Eagles. You can do that in New Jersey?"

"Of course you can," she laughed.

I was shocked. I never would have thought that Mrs. Bailey lived in Jersey. On our class trips she always wore a Phillies cap. She didn't even have an accent!

"Did you move to New Jersey from Philadelphia?"

"Sure did," she said.

"Were you mad?"

"Not at all. New Jersey has a lot of great places and things to do. In fact, it's closer to Philadelphia than most places in Pennsylvania."

I had never thought about it that way, but it was true. New Jersey was closer to Philadelphia than cities like Gettysburg, Harrisburg, and Pittsburgh. But I was used to Philly and I hated change.

"Okay, Nick, this is what we're going

to do. When you go home, make a list of everything you're going to miss about Philadelphia and I'll make a list of all of the good things in New Jersey. And when you finish your list, don't forget to do pages 145-147 in your math book, sleepyhead."

I felt myself starting to smile. Maybe because I felt better knowing Mrs. Bailey lived in New Jersey or maybe because I loved a challenge.

"Alright, get out of here," she said. "You have alot of work to do."

"Bye," I said, gathering my books.

When I walked out the door, everyone was waiting for me, including Timmy.

"Nick, Nick are you in trouble? Did you get detention?" Timmy asked, as usual, two inches from my face.

"No," I said as I pushed him out of my way.

"So Rip Van Wrinkled, what happened

to you?" asked Joey Grapes, noticing the sleeve marks on my face.

I still wasn't ready to tell my friends about moving and decided to keep quiet.

"Nothing's wrong. I fell asleep. It happens."

"Could it have anything to do with your family moving to New Hampshire?" Gino Pie asked, with a huge grin. The only thing Gino loved more than a juicy pie was juicy gossip.

My mouth dropped. I turned my head and glared at Timmy.

"What?" Timmy asked, looking at the ground. "They dragged it out of me."

"And it was real hard," said Boots. "We asked him what was up?"

"Good job," I told my shadow.

"So what's the deal?" asked Benny Bones. "Are you really moving to New Hampshire?"

"No."

"I told you Timmy had it wrong," Joey Grapes said. "There's no way Nicky Fifth would leave Philadelphia, huh Nick?"

"Actually, we might be moving, but not to New Hampshire. We might move to New Jersey."

"Hey, first Mikey Jones, now you," said Freddie Dragon.

Freddie was so convinced that Mikey Jones was real, I almost forgot that I made him up.

"What are they giving away in New Jersey?" Gino Pie asked.

"Pie," I said sarcastically. "Wanna come?"

"Seriously," Joey Grapes interrupted, "you're really moving to Jersey? Why?"

"It looks like it," I said. "My dad wants to live in the country and he found a house he likes."

"That sucks," said Boots. "It won't be the same without you."

The whole mood of the group changed. As we walked home, no one said much, except Timmy. He told everyone about the house. He actually seemed excited, but then again, why wouldn't he be? I was his best friend and I'd be right there in New Jersey with him.

When we got to my house, we just stood there in silence. This was exactly what I had been dreading. None of us knew what to say. Everyone, was staring at me, even my shadow. After a few minutes of staring back, I decided to make a move.

"See you tomorrow," Boots said, as I walked up the steps.

"Later," I mumbled.

64

Chapter Seven

The Sunday Clipper

I walked in the house with my shadow right behind me. On the one hand, I wanted to twist him into a pretzel for telling everyone we were moving. On the other hand, I almost felt relieved that everyone knew. I still didn't feel any better about moving, but it was one less thing to worry about.

I started my math homework right away. I wanted to have plenty of time, after dinner, to work on my list. Sitting at the kitchen table, I opened up my math book.

Before I could find a pencil, my grandfather walked in.

"Grandma and I missed you at breakfast today."

In the morning, things were so hectic in my house, that we usually ate breakfast at my grandparents. I was so tired this morning, I had forgotten all about it.

"I figured I better get used to not eating at your house anymore," I said, in another attempt to make him feel guilty and let me move in. I was hoping my absence left such a void at breakfast that he came up to beg me to move in.

"Really?" he asked. "We were hoping you would keep coming for breakfast until you move."

Until I move. That didn't sound like begging, I thought.

"I was running late," I said. "I didn't sleep very well."

"Did you think about the move?"

In my opinion, that was the most ridiculous question ever asked. How could I think about anything else? Except for my baseball dream, which I was still mad about not finishing, this move was all I thought about.

"Yeah," I said, pretending to start my homework.

"Do you feel any better?" he asked.

"No, Pop. In fact, I don't think I'll ever be happy again. Timmy told my friends today and no one even knew what to say."

"I suspect that they were probably shocked. I'm sure they didn't want to say how they really feel because they didn't want to make you feel bad," he said.

"Well, I don't think it matters. Either way, I feel bad."

My grandfather was the kind of guy who knew when to push and when to back off. It was one of the things I liked best about him. He saw that I wasn't in the mood to talk, so he backed off.

"Well, I'm going to give your grandmother a hand downstairs," he said as he walked toward the door. "Should we expect you for breakfast tomorrow?"

"I guess."

I finished my homework and decided to watch television until dinner. I flipped through the stations and found the New Jersey Network News. I was hoping they would have a breaking story from the Governor's Office. Maybe they just passed a law so no one else could move to New Jersey.

Instead, they were interviewing a farmer. By the time dinner was ready, I had learned two things, New Jersey does have farms and it's called the Garden State.

That's it, I thought. My father wants us to move there because it's called the Garden State. Suddenly, it all made sense. My father, whose whole life revolved around fruits and vegetables, was dragging us out of Philadelphia so his license plate would say Garden State. I felt myself getting mad all over again.

I kept watching. The anchorman said the weather forecast was next. It was strange, but they were having the same weather as Philadelphia. It must have been a coincidence.

"Nicky, Timmy, Maggie, it's time for dinner," my mom called.

I could smell the peanut butter as Maggie walked by the family room. I often wondered how a four year old could always smell like peanut butter. Maybe she took peanut butter bubble baths.

"Nick, Nick, are you coming? Mom said it's time for dinner. Are you coming?" Timmy asked, again two inches from my face.

He was amazing. You could set your watch by him. He couldn't go more than ten minutes without seeing what I was up to. We shared a bedroom for as long as I could remember and I sometimes heard him call my name in his sleep.

"I'm coming," I said. "I'm coming."

We all sat down for dinner and I already knew we would talk about the house. I just figured it would start after they asked us how our days went.

"So, I talked to the realtor," my dad began.

I was wrong. We would lead off with the new house. I guess knowing how everyone's day went could wait.

"Margorie said we can move in next month!"

"Really?" my mom said. "Do you think we can be ready?"

"Well, it'll be tough, but I know we can do it. There's only one problem and it's not a big problem. I guess it's just an issue."

"What is it, Jim?" my mom asked, stopping in her tracks.

"Well, the house is going to cost a little more than I figured, with closing costs and everything, so we're going to have to tighten our belts to make this work."

With that, Maggie jumped up from the table, ran to her bedroom and returned with a pink belt.

"Here daddy," she said, handing it to him. "You can have my belt."

My parents started laughing, then Timmy and even Emma. Even though she didn't understand why she was laughing, Emma was a follower. You could just, out of the clear blue sky, start laughing and Emma would giggle for hours.

"No, sweetie." my mom said, hugging

Maggie. "That's not what Daddy meant. It's just an expression."

I couldn't take it any more. My father just announced that we would have to make sacrifices to move to New Jersey and everyone was laughing about it.

"Exactly how tight?" I asked.

"What?" my dad said, still cracking up.

"Exactly how tight will the belt have to be?" I repeated, rather impatiently.

"Oh," my dad said. "Well, nothing drastic, we'll just have to be more careful with our money. We'll have to cut out some of the extras for a while."

Cut out some of the extras? I thought. We already sneak 3 pounds of popcorn and a twelve pack of soda in the diaper bag when we go to the movies. When we go out to eat, we eat at 4:30 with all of the old people because dad says it's better for digestion. He didn't know that I know it's cheaper to order the early-bird specials. We never ordered dessert out because my dad said it's more fun to eat popsicles in the grocery store parking lot. What could we possibly tighten?

"What extras?" I asked, growing angrier by the minute. I couldn't wait to hear what my father considered to be an *extra*.

"Well, for starters, you kids could bring your lunch to school instead of buying it there."

"That's not a problem," my mom said. "The girls and I could make them at night in our brand new kitchen!"

I rolled my eyes. So much for relax, this is just a phase.

"Another way we could save some money is by buying generic food," my dad suggested.

"We're not Jewish," Timmy interjected.

"Not kosher food, Tim, generic food. It tastes the same, it just looks different than the brand names."

"I don't get it," Timmy groaned.

"Let me explain," I said in my most sarcastic tone. "Instead of the foods you are used to, you'll be eating Circle-O's for breakfast and drinking lemon-lime soda with dinner."

"Believe it or not, Nick, many generic foods are made at the same plants as the brand names. They just don't waste money on advertising. It'll be fine. I bet you won't even notice."

"What else?" I asked.

"Well, I thought we should start clipping coupons. My store doubles coupons up to one dollar and I'm sure the savings could add up. In fact, since you're the oldest Nick, maybe that will be your job. Every Sunday, I'll pick up a few extra papers and you can cut out the coupons for me. It'll be fun!"

Or maybe they could sell their oldest

son to a nice family that lives in Philadelphia.

Chapter Eight

There's Two Sides To Every River

The rest of dinner was spent listening to my dad think of ways for us to make sacrifices. He suggested sending more e-mails to lower the phone bill, wearing sweaters in the winter to lower the heating bill, and my personal favorite, wearing our sneakers and clothes until they wear out. Before dinner, I thought he was losing his mind. Now I was sure.

When he finished thinking up ways to make our lives unbearable, I went up to my room. I sat on my bed with a notebook and drew a line down the center of the paper. Before I could finish drawing the line, my shadow entered.

"Nick, I was looking for you. Where'd you go?"

"Where do you think?"

"Good one," he said, staring at the notebook.

"Do you need something?" I asked.

Of course, I knew the answer to that question. He didn't need anything. He never needed anything. He just liked to be wherever I was, constantly breathing down my neck.

"I just wanted see what you were doing."

"Why don't you go play with Maggie," I suggested.

"No way," he objected. "She's a pain in the neck. She never leaves me alone."

"I can't imagine," I said, rolling my eyes.

I decided to treat him like a bee. They say if you ignore a bee, it'll fly away. Maybe it would work with Timmy.

I started working on my list. One side was for things that I loved about Philadelphia, the other side was for things Mrs. Bailey loved about New Jersey. I jotted down some ideas:

1. The Liberty Bell
2. Independence Hall
3. South Street
4. Ben Franklin's House
5. Penn's Landing
6. The Philadelphia Zoo
7. The Italian Market
8. Pat's & Gino's Cheesesteaks
9. Fairmount Park
10. Rittenhouse Square
11. Olde City
12. Grandmom and Pop
13. Joey Grapes
14. Gino Pie

15. Bobby Boots
16. Crazy John
17. Benny Bones
18. Freddie
19. My house
20. Philadelphia

After 30 minutes, I had created a list of twenty reasons why I did not want to leave Philadelphia. I looked at my list with pride and sadness. I was happy that I could show Mrs. Bailey, in black and white, why I didn't want to move. At the same time, though, looking at the list made me start missing Philadelphia and I hadn't even left.

I put the list in my backpack and got ready for bed. I wondered what Mrs. Bailey was putting on her list. I couldn't think of one thing. I figured she might even call in sick because she was embarrassed by her list. I wouldn't have been surprised if, after making her list, she made her husband move back to Philadelphia.

Even though I didn't sleep very well, I woke up early the next morning and went down to my grandparents.

"Good morning, sweetie," my grandmom said as she flipped the French toast in the frying pan.

"Good morning."

"Well, look who it is," my grandfather said as he walked into the kitchen. "How are we today?"

"Terrible," I said as I poured myself some orange juice. "How are you?"

"To be honest," said my Grandmom, " we wish you were happier about moving."

"If wishes came true, I wouldn't be moving."

"Give him some time, dear," Pop told her. "Give the boy some time to adjust."

Before I could respond, the door

opened.

"Nick, Nick, where did you go? Don't leave for school without me."

"Wouldn't dream of it," I said, as sarcastic as possible.

In a few minutes my whole family was downstairs. I decided to eat fast and leave early for school. The suspense was killing me. I wanted to see Mrs. Bailey's list.

"Get your stuff, Timmy. I'm leaving."

"But it's too early," he complained.

"Then walk by yourself," I shot back.

"Alright, alright. I'm coming," he said, as if there was any doubt that he would be right behind me.

We walked to the back of the building so I could scan the faculty parking lot. There it was, Mrs. Bailey's green van. I entered the building and went right to her homeroom.

"Good morning, Nick," Mrs. Bailey said, looking over her glasses.

I always wondered why she even wore glasses. She spent part of the day looking over the glasses, part of the day wearing them on the top of her head, and the rest of the day looking for them. She usually found them on top of her head.

"Good morning," I said.

"Well, how did you make out with your list?" she asked.

"Fine."

"Don't be shy. Let's see it," she said.

I pulled it out, sure that she would be impressed.

I placed my list on her desk.

"You know what," she said. "Why don't you read something off of yours and I'll try to read something comparable off of mine."

"Okay," I said, almost feeling sorry for her.

We held our lists like two cowboys ready to draw. For a quick moment, I felt nervous, but I didn't know why. I was positive that she couldn't have much. We went back and forth like two tennis players in a championship match. I started out with a national treasure.

"The Liberty Bell."

"Good one," she said with a smile. "The Old Barracks in Trenton. George Washington's troops stayed there."

Man, I hadn't thought of that one.

"Independence Hall, it's very historical," I said, raising one eyebrow.

"Washington's Crossing, I'm sure you've heard of it. It's just where George Washington crossed the Delaware and the turning point of the Revolution," she said, raising her eyebrow.

I went with South Street, stores and restaurants, a great place to walk around.

She shot right back with Lambertville, stores and restaurants, a great place to walk around.

Obviously, she had put some thought into this, but she couldn't go on much longer.

"Ben Franklin's House, it's a colonial treasure."

"The William Trent House. It, too, is a colonial treasure," she said, raising the other eyebrow.

"Penn's Landing on the beautiful Delaware River."

"Ferries to Penn's Landing on the beautiful Delaware River."

Geez! I forgot that New Jersey was on the other side of the river. Moving along.

"The Philadelphia Zoo, a wonderful collection of animals from all over the world."

"The New Jersey State Aquarium, a wonderful collection of animals from all over the world."

I couldn't believe it. She had something for every one of my ideas. She must have had help, probably her New Jersey husband.

"The Italian Market, there's nothing like it in the world."

"Chambersburg, New Jersey's Little Italy. You should drive down some day."

"Maybe when I have a license," I said with the kind of sarcasim reserved for my shadow. I had to stop and take a breath. Pretty soon the only things I would have to offer would be Gino Pie and Bobby Boots.

"Okay, Gino's Steaks and Pat's Steaks, the best cheesesteaks in the World. Name me one food that people will drive for miles to find."

"Easy, DeLorenzo's Tomato Pies, on Hudson Street in Trenton, it's what pizza dreams about. When you're old enough to drive, stop by and say hi to Sam."

Stop by and say hi to Sam? Now, she

was just getting cocky.

"Fairmount Park."

"Six Flags Amusement Park and Safari."

Ouch, she got me on that one. I forgot about Six Flags. She had to be running out of things soon.

"Rittenhouse Square."

"The Jersey Shore, including Atalntic City and all of the other great boardwalks."

Man, she must not have slept last night.

"Olde City."

"The mountains, only if you enjoy hiking, skiing, snowboarding, and sledding."

And here we were, Mrs. Bailey with her eight foot list and I was down to listing family and friends. Then I thought about it and wondered what could possibly compare with family and friends? Suddenly, it hit me. Nothing, absolutely nothing could compare to good friends and family. Pop says that all of the time. She would never be able to beat it. I decided to go for it.

"Grandmom and Grandpop," I said rather smugly.

"Grandmom and Grandpop," she rebutted. "You'll have your grandparents no matter where you live."

"Joey Grapes, Gino Pie, Bobby Boots, Crazy John, Benny Bones, and Freddie."

"Okay," she said. "I'll give you all of them except, maybe Freddie. Are you sure you want him on your list of things you'll miss?"

For a second, I thought she was serious, until she started smiling.

"I'm kidding, I'm kidding," she said. "Actually, you'll have your old friends, plus you'll have new friends."

I was hoping she was at the end of her list because I only had two left.

"My house, I don't want to leave my house."

"Your new house. I have a feeling that you'll really enjoy having more space to run and play and even hide from Timmy!"

I hated how every adult said I would love having more room to run and play. It made me sound like a golden retriever. On the other hand, hiding from my shadow wasn't bad.

"Okay, here's my last one, Philadelphia."

"Fair enough," she said, "but that was my last one also."

"No fair," I said. "You can't use Philadelphia on your list. I'm leaving Philadelphia."

"On the contrary," she said. "Philadelphia is not floating away and neither are you. You'll just be on the other side of the bridge. Your grandparents live here and so do many of your friends. You can come and go whenever you want and I'm sure you'll always have a place to stay."

"But I won't be a Philadelphian anymore, I'll be a New Jerseyan."

"That's where you're wrong," she said. "You'll always be a Philadelphian, no matter where you roam. Remember, you can take the boy out of Philadelphia, but you can't take the Philadelphia out of the boy."

Chapter Nine

Nervous Breakdown in Aisle Six

The next two weeks almost seemed normal. The newness of the house was wearing off and my parents occasionally talked about other things. There were even times when I actually forgot that we were moving. But then, I would remember and it would sting all over again.

By the beginning of April, things picked up. My parents were constantly talking about mortgage rates and interest. Our Sunday rides turned into furniture expeditions.   Instead of mooing at cows, we sat on leather couches. We went from store to store, walking aisle after aisle.

The worst part was entering a store. I watched other people walk into these stores and the salespeople would trip over themselves trying to be the first to give them their business card. When we walked in and they saw four kids, they ran for the hills. Occasionally, some new salesman would venture over and ask if we needed anything. To that question, my parents consistently gave the same answer.

"No, thank you, we're just looking."

That, I believe, may have been why I was beginning to dread Sunday on Monday mornings. We spent hours and hours looking at tables and chairs and lamps and we never bought anything. It wouldn't have felt like such a monumental waste of time if, for once, we had actually bought something. I would have been happy with a doorknob.

At one point, I convinced myself that they weren't buying anything because they weren't sure if they would go through with moving. Then I remembered my dad's speech about tightening the belt. He already had me clipping coupons, so I knew he meant it.

By mid-April we received a phone call from our realtor. I only heard my father's end of the conversation, but I was pretty sure that it wasn't good news.

"Oh, sure we understand," my dad told Margorie. "I guess these things happen."

Could this be the answer to my prayers, I thought. It would have been too good to be true, but I had been praying that the Woodward's would change their minds about moving to California. Maybe they read about the earthquakes and mudslides and decided to take their chances in New

Jersey. My dad hung up and I held my breath.

"Erin, come here for a second," my dad hollered.

"I'll be right there."

While he waited for my mom, I pretended to read my social studies notes. From the corner of my eye, I could see my dad staring out the window.

"What is it, dear?" my mom asked.

"That was Margorie on the phone. She just spoke to the Woodward's realtor and there's a problem."

"Oh, no," my mom said, sitting down.

Oh, yes, I thought.

"It seems that the Woodward's house in California isn't ready and they would like to stay until the end of June. What do you think?"

"That's all?" my mom asked with a big smile. "That would actually be great. The kids could finish out the school year and I'll be on my summer vacation when it's time to pack and move."

Oh, no, I thought. This wasn't bad news.

"Are you sure?" he said. "I know how much you want to move in. I thought you'd be upset when I told you."

"A month ago, we had no plans on moving," she said, smiling. "If anything, this makes me much more relaxed about the whole situation."

"I am so relieved," my dad said as he gave her a big hug. "I was really afraid that if we waited, you might change your mind."

"Not a chance," she laughed, giving him a kiss on the nose.

I couldn't believe it. Not only were we still moving, but ever since my dad found this house, they were hugging all of the time. It's not like they didn't get along before the house, but now it felt like they were dating. I found it very annoying.

"Nick, good news," my dad said, just noticing that I was on their date. "You can finish school and your baseball season in Philadelphia. How's that sound?"

"A dream come true," I said with a fake-smile as I walked over and sarcastically kissed him on the nose. "I have goose bumps."

And with that, I went to bed. I hoped they would see how ridiculous they had been acting, but I realized that my sarcasm went right over their heads.

"Good night, honey," they hollered upstairs.

"Whatever," I responded.

I sat at my desk and thought about what had just happened. Even though I would never admit it, I realized my dad's news was kind of good. I definitely wanted to finish out the year in my own school and now I could pitch the whole season. Still, knowing that we were eventually moving made it impossible to be really happy.

Two minutes after I got in bed, Timmy walked in.

"Nick,-Nick, I was looking all over for you."

I closed my eyes and pretended to be asleep. Even with my eyes closed, I could feel him staring at me. He had to be an inch away from my face.

"Nick-Nick, are you asleep?' he asked as he pulled my right eyelid open.

"Yes," I said, looking at him with the one eye.

"Oh," he said, letting go and walking away.

I was in such a bad mood, that I decided it was best not to talk to anyone, especially Timmy. He really wasn't a bad kid, he just had a way of grinding my nerves. Besides being my shadow, he had an annoying habit of always saying my name twice. It was as if he thought my name was Nick, Nick.

I rolled on my side and pretended to sleep until, at some point, which I don't remember, I fell asleep. The next morning, my dad came in and woke me up for my game.

"Wake up, slugger," he said. "You have a big game at eleven o'clock."

"What time is it?" I asked.

"Eight o'clock," he answered.

"Eight o'clock? Why are you waking me up so early?" If he was waking me up to go furniture shopping, I would have screamed.

"I thought we could do some grocery shopping before your game," he said, holding the coupon organizer. "If we're going to save money, I'll need you to help me with these coupons."

I was hoping he was joking, but he wasn't.

"Grab a quick shower, get your uniform on, and we'll go to the store before your game."

This could not be happening, I thought. He wanted me to go food shopping and hold his coupon organizer, wearing my uniform, on game day?

"Take Tim-Tim," I said, rolling over.

"I can't. He's going furniture shopping with your mom."

"I'll be right down," I said, dragging myself out of bed. I figured it was better than furniture shopping. At least I knew we'd buy something.

It took five minutes in the grocery store to realize I was wrong. It wasn't bad enough that I had to shop in my uniform, but my dad turned into an army general. He had a list in one hand and the circular in the other.

He handed me the organizer and told me to be careful not to drop any coupons.

"These coupons are money," he warned. "Each one of those is double the money it says."

If he told me once, he told me eighty times. I felt like I was carrying a pot of gold. Unfortunately, his constant warnings weren't the worst of it. As we worked the store, aisle by aisle, he would name the next item on the list. Apparently, it was my job to see if we had any coupons for that item. Then we would search for the right brand and flavor and size.

The cart was filling up very slowly. Occasionally, I would hold up something that we bought every week. My father would look at me and ask the same question.

"Do you have a coupon for it?"

If we didn't, he bought the generic version. When the cashier handed my dad the receipt, she smiled and told him he saved

$34.00.

He never looked prouder.

Chapter Ten

Room With A View, Door With A Lock

By the time May rolled around, the question wasn't if we were going to move, but when. My mom had already started throwing things away and every night at dinner she would say the same thing.

"You just can't imagine how many things you accumulate until you move."

In an effort to reduce the clutter, she began to throw away more things than she packed. I started to monitor the garbage bags. Most of the bags were filled with actual garbage, but sometimes I found things that weren't.

One day, while Joey Grapes and I were sitting on the steps, she placed eight bags on the curb. When I opened the first bag, I saw a box with my baseball cards. I grabbed the box and ran in the house.

"Mom, what are you doing? You threw away my baseball cards."

"What?" she asked, wiping the sweat from her forehead.

"My baseball cards," I said, holding out the box.

"Oh, did you want to keep them?"

Did I want to keep them?

"These will be worth big money one day. Do you have any idea how long it took me to save all of these cards?"

"Oh," she said. "Sorry."

Sorry? That was it. If I didn't open that bag, they would have been gone forever.

I started to wonder what else she had thrown out.

I went back outside and showed Joey Grapes the box. As we looked at the cards, he started to talk about the move. It felt weird, since this was a topic that never came up with my friends. It was probably the reason I enjoyed spending more time with them instead of my family.

"Do you know when you're leaving?" he asked.

"I don't know. They said the end of June."

"That's not too bad. At least you can pitch us to the championship game."

"I guess," I said.

While it was a relief that my friends didn't talk about it 24 hours a day, I wondered if they even cared that I was moving.

"Look, Nick," Joey Grapes said, "we know you're mad about leaving, but it's not that bad."

"Not that bad?" I shot back. "You get mad when your mom puts yellow cheese on your sandwiches. How would you like to leave your friends, your school, and Philadelphia?"

"First of all, I hate yellow cheese and she knows that. Second of all, I wouldn't want to leave, but I'm different than you. I don't have grandparents who live in the neighborhood."

"What do you mean?"

"None of us are worried about you leaving because we know we'll still see you all of the time. You know you'll be at your grandparents all the time. Now, if your grandparents were moving, then we'd be worried."

"Yeah, but it still won't be the same."

"In September not much will be the same anyway," he insisted.

"What are you talking about?"

"Are you kidding?" he asked. "We'll all be going to middle school. Have you seen the size of that place? There's like a thousand kids there. We all won't be together like we are now. My older brother says you meet alot of new kids and make alot of new friends."

"Yeah, but we're tight. That never would have changed."

"I don't think so," he said, as he read the stats on the back of a card. "My brother had a tight group of friends, and they still hang out, but it's different. They have other friends, too."

"So you don't think this is bad?"

"Don't get me wrong," he laughed, " you couldn't pay me to move to New Jersey, but other than that it's not that bad."

We didn't speak for a while. We just looked through the box of cards. As I read the stats, I thought about what he had said. It was like talking to my grandfather. At least, I knew why my friends didn't think it was a big deal. Maybe it wasn't.

When Joey left, I went up to my room and looked over Mrs. Bailey's list. I hated to admit it, but New Jersey did have some cool places. And Joey Grapes was right, as long as my grandparents stayed put, I could visit as often as I wanted.

I stayed in my room, waiting for my mom to call me to dinner. When I noticed it was after seven o'clock, I began to panic. Maybe they did realize how sarcastic I had become and decided to stop feeding me. I went downstairs expecting to see everyone sitting at the table. When I walked into the kitchen, I didn't see anyone. I went out front and saw everyone sitting on the steps.

"Are we eating tonight?" I asked.

"Your mom lost track of time with all

of the packing," dad explained. "We're just waiting for the pizza guy."

While I wouldn't exactly call what my mom was doing packing, I was happy to hear that we ordered a pizza. Just as I wondered how pizza for six people would fit into our new budget, my dad showed me a coupon.

"Look at this, Nick. On Tuesdays, if you buy two pizzas, you get two free. I saw it in the paper today. Not bad, eh?"

"That's great, dad," I said, trying not to roll my eyes.

While my mom's new hobby was throwing things away, my dad's had become showing people his grocery store receipts. When anyone came over he'd pull out a receipt and point to the line that read Total Saved. Last week was his biggest haul. The bill should have been $124.00, but he only paid $78.00. I was waiting to see it framed and hanging on the wall.

With my mom teaching all day and packing all night, when we ate and what we ate became as predictable as the weather. If it wasn't for Grandmom sending up entire meals, we would have moved to New Jersey looking like pizzas.

Dinner wasn't the only thing to change. As we neared the end of May, our house looked like a warehouse. Boxes were stacked everywhere. Walking from one room to the other was like walking through a corn maze. But the best change happened while we were shopping for furniture.

"See anything you'd like for your new bedroom?" asked my dad. "We'll put the furniture we have now in Timmy's room."

Timmy's room! Those words were music to my ears. I had a feeling that the best part of having my own room would be the door.

Chapter Eleven

Ed Has A Younger Brother?

We officially moved into our new house on July 3rd. Ironically, we had to wait because we still needed furniture. After two months of dragging us to furniture stores, it took my parents one day, without kids, to select everything.

Once the store delivered all of the furniture, my mom made arrangements for the movers to bring the rest of our stuff. They promised to arrive on Wednesday morning by 8:30 am.. Sitting in the middle of the cardboard maze, I hoped they were right. With everything we owned either packed, wrapped, or at the dump, things became less than comfortable.

At 7:00 am, I heard a faint tapping on my window. I assumed it was a bird, since we lived on the second floor. A few minutes later, the tapping became louder and faster. I rolled over and tried to ignore it.

Suddenly, a rock, the size of a tennis ball, came crashing through my window. I jumped out of bed and looked through the hole that used to be my window. On the ground, I saw Freddie standing there with his mouth open.

"Dude, what are you doing?" I whispered.

"It was too early to call and I didn't want to knock and wake anyone up."

"Good job," I said, rolling my eyes.

"Nick, Nick, what was that?" Timmy

screamed as he jumped out of his bed.

"Shhh," I said, motioning him to be quiet. "Freddie broke the window."

Before I could tell him not to wake up my parents, they were standing in my door-way.

"What was that noise?" my dad asked as he opened the door.

"What noise?" I asked, trying to block the hole with my body.

Too late. My mom looked at the floor and saw pieces of glass everywhere.

"Don't move, Nick. You have bare feet and you're surrounded by glass," she cautioned.

"I'll get the broom and the dustpan," my dad said, running to the kitchen.

I don't know how I made it to the win-dow without cutting my feet, but there was no way I could repeat the trick. I had already stood there for several minutes, without moving, when I heard my dad yelling.

"Erin, where's the broom and dust-pan?"

My mom didn't answer. She was biting her lower lip and grimacing.

"Erin," he hollered louder. "Where are they?"

"I packed them."

"You packed the broom and dust pan?"

"Yes."

"Why would you pack them when we still have to clean?"

"I don't know, I packed everything."

I hated to interrupt, but I couldn't feel my legs anymore.

"Uh, mom," I began to say.

Before I could finish, she threw my sneakers at me. Unfortunately, she didn't warn me that she was throwing two sneakers at the same time and one went out the window.

"Ouch!" a voice screamed from down

below.

I turned around and saw Boots rubbing his head.

"Who screamed?" she asked in a panic.

"It's just Boots."

"Bobby Boots? What is he doing here?"

"Rubbing his head," I said, amused by the path my morning had taken.

"You alright?" I asked him, as I slipped on one sneaker and hopped out of the glass.

"Yeah," he said holding my sneaker.

I went downstairs and we sat on the steps. Bobby Boots handed me my shoe. Ten minutes later, the rest of the gang showed up. Gino Pie's mom had sent a basket with homemade muffins and cookies. Joey Grape's mom sent over some orange juice and paper cups. This worked out well since my mom packed or threw away almost everything from the kitchen.

Crazy John brought a tennis ball. We started tossing it around.

"What time is the truck coming?" he asked.

"Around 8:30. But I'm not going today."

"You're not?" everyone asked together.

"No, my grandmother said we can stay at her house for a few days while my mom gets things ready."

"Cool," Gino said, nodding his head.

"What do you want to do?" Joey Grapes asked.

"I have to look for the truck."

"Do you need help carrying the boxes?" asked Bones.

"We'll help," announced Freddie.

"I think you helped enough," I said, laughing. "Plus, I think my mom and dad want the professional movers to load everything."

By 9:00, the truck still hadn't arrived. I told my dad I would call him when it pulled up, but he looked out the front door every time a car drove down the street. We were still tossing the ball.

Just before 10:00, the truck pulled up. It was the oldest truck I had ever seen. The only thing older than the truck, was the driver.

It had already taken him five minutes to get out of the truck when he realized he had forgotten his clipboard. Five minutes later, he walked up to the house, clipboard in hand.

"Is this the Abruzzi house?," he asked slowly.

"Yes," I answered.

"Come again," he said.

"Yes," I said louder.

"Did you say yes?" he asked.

"Yes," we shouted together.

"Alright, alright. No need to holler!"

I ran inside to tell my dad that the truck had arrived. He came out and looked at the old guy in front of our house. The side of the truck read:

**Ed's Reliable Moving Service
Established 1953**

My dad looked scared, especially when he didn't see anyone else come out of the truck.

"Good morning," he said. "Are you, Ed?"

"No thanks," he patted his stomach. "I already had some eggs."

"No, are you Ed?" my dad asked slower and louder.

"Sure am. Are you all packed up?"

"Yes, everything is upstairs. Do you have anyone else to help you?"

"No, my older brother is having a bypass this week and my younger brother took off to go fishing. Why, is your stuff heavy?"

My dad's mouth dropped. Of course our stuff was heavy. We were moving a whole house, not cotton balls.

The rest of us couldn't take our eyes off of him. He had a dirty baseball hat, coveralls, and a cigar hanging out of his mouth. I wasn't an expert, but I was sure he wouldn't be able to lift anything heavier than Emma.

"Ed, I'll be right back," my dad said running into the house.

"Nice to meet you, Jack," he responded.

I followed my dad inside. I knew he was looking for my mom and I didn't want to miss this conversation. I could guarantee that they wouldn't be hugging when my dad was through.

"Erin, where did you find the movers?"

"In the yellow pages," she answered, not sensing there was a problem. "They were the most reasonable and guess what? There was a coupon!"

"Well, did they mention that the company was 50 years old and the mover was 75?"

"What are you talking about?" my mom asked.

"Erin, there is one old truck out front, with one old man. How do you suggest we get everything in the truck?"

"I don't know," she snapped. "The woman I spoke with said it would be Ed and his two brothers."

"Well, his older brother is having a bypass and his younger brother went fishing."

"Now what? It's too late to find another mover and I can't let him help me move the heavy things."

"Stay right here," I said.

I ran outside and asked my friends if their dad's were home. Boots' father was off and Crazy John's dad was on vacation.

"Alright," I directed. "You guys go see if you can get them to come over. The rest of you, come with me."

We walked upstairs and heard my parents arguing.

As soon as they saw us, they stopped.

"Okay, Boots and Crazy John went home to get their dads," I announced. "The rest of us will help load the boxes."

My mom and dad stopped and stared at me. They seemed shocked. I think they expected me to enjoy that everything was going wrong. I actually surprised myself that I wasn't enjoying it.

"Really?" my mom asked. "That's so

nice of you guys."

"No problem," said Joey Grapes. "Just tell us what you need loaded."

"Only if Freddie promises to stay away from anything breakable!" my dad said with a smirk.

"Good one, Mr. Abruzzi," laughed Freddie.

"I'm not joking," my father told him.

A few minutes later, Crazy John returned with his dad and his older brother. Boots showed up with his dad and his uncle. My dad shook their hands and thanked them for saving us.

"No problem, Jim," said Boots' dad. "We'll have you loaded in no time."

We started an assembly line, with the kids passing the boxes down the steps and onto the truck. When it was time to move the heavy pieces of furniture, the bigger guys took over and we held the doors.

As we loaded the truck, Ed was very helpful. Every three seconds he would share pearls of wisdom from his 50 years as a mover.

"Watch your step. Lift with your back. Watch your head. Don't carry so much, make two trips."

"Where did you get this guy?" asked Crazy John's uncle.

"Long story," my dad said, obviously embarrassed to tell anyone about the coupon.

When the truck was loaded, everyone sat on the step and drank the lemonade my grandmother had set out, including Ed. We all felt pretty good about loading the truck until Gino Pie asked the question no one had thought about.

"Who's going to unload all of this stuff?'

Thankfully, everyone that helped load the truck came over to unload it, too. My friends really liked my new house and asked when they could sleep over. Even better, they never noticed the name of my street. I still had time to come up with a plan.

By 9:00 pm, I was back on the Ben Franklin Bridge, excited to spend my first night at my grandparents, as a visitor.

Chapter Twelve

No Igloos Here

The rest of the summer wasn't too bad. I spent a lot of time at my grandparents house and hanging out with my friends. I met some of the kids in my new neighborhood and they seemed decent enough. My biggest worry was going to a new school, especially a middle school.

Looking back, I worried much more than I needed to. Every sixth grader looked pretty freaked out. We roamed the halls with schedules in our hands, trying to find our next class while dodging the seventh and eighth graders. I ended up in the wrong classes three times during the first week. The funniest thing was how many people asked me for directions.

Because eight elementary schools filtered into the middle school, no one realized I was new. *Everyone was new.* By the end of the first week, I had everything under control, even riding a school bus. After all those years of making fun of the kids who stood in their driveways, waiting for big yellow buses, I was now one of them. I hated to admit it, but it wasn't too bad.

At first, I didn't really talk to anyone. I never thought I was shy, but I found out I was. After a couple of weeks I decided I better start making some new friends.

I looked at the kids on my bus and figured I should start there since they lived in my neighborhood. Instead of sitting by myself, I sat down next to a kid wearing a

Flyers hat.

"Hey," I said.

"What's up?" he asked.

"Not much," I answered. I wished I had something cool to say, but I couldn't think of anything.

"Did you just move here?" he asked.

"Yeah."

"Where from?"

"Philly," I answered.

"Cool. You ever catch any Flyers games?"

"All the time," I exaggerated.

"I've only been to one. What's your name?"

"Nicky Abruzzi. My friends call me Nicky Fifth."

"I'm Tommy Rizzo, My friends call me T-Bone."

The bus stopped at my corner and we

both got off.

"You moved into the Woodwards old house?" he asked.

"Yeah," I answered. "Where do you live?"

"Around the corner, on Petunia."

"Oh," I said, making a face.

"Tell me about it," he said. "You play baseball?"

"Pitcher," I said.

"We're playing at the field in an hour, if you want to come."

"Alright," I said.

"I'll meet you at your house around 4:00."

I couldn't believe it. They had nicknames and a baseball field. For the first time since I moved to New Jersey, I was excited.

At 4:00, the doorbell rang. I opened the door and saw Tommy and two other kids. He introduced me to Joey Dirt and Frankie

Skids. I didn't know why they had those nicknames and I didn't care. They asked me to pitch and I met six other kids from the neighborhood.

When I went home that night, my parents noticed my mood was different. For the first time in months, I was smiling. I told them about my day and they seemed very happy. My mom confessed that they were really concerned about me. I told her that they didn't need to worry.

Later, that night, I e-mailed Joey Grapes. He filled me in on everything I had been missing in Philly and asked how Jersey was. I shocked myself when I told him it was pretty good.

Over the next couple of months, things got better. I finally learned my way around school, and made some new friends. Every couple of weeks I would stay at my grandparents house and hangout with my old friends.

My dad continued to bring me to the grocery store and after a while, I even enjoyed it. With so many kids in the family, it was one of the only times I could hang out with my dad alone.

While Emma was too little to be happy or sad about moving, Timmy and Maggie seemed to love our new house and neighborhood. With all of the kids around, Timmy became less of a shadow and more of a little brother.

My mom, the one who told me she had no intentions of moving, probably loved the house more than anyone. If you needed her, you didn't need to look farther than the kitchen. It was months before we ordered our first pizza.

One night, after e-mailing my old friends, I remembered my grandfather telling me not to move my igloo south. It took a while, but it suddenly made sense. If I was going to be happy in New Jersey, I couldn't try to turn it into Philadelphia. I had to accept the fact that even though many things were similar, it was still different. I couldn't expect my new friends to act like my old ones and I couldn't be upset that things weren't the same.

I decided to let my grandfather know that he was probably right and I sent him an e-mail:

Hey Pop,
I just wanted to let you know that you were right. Moving to New Jersey wasn't the end of the world and I finally understand what you meant when you told me not to move my igloo south.
Nick

An hour later, I noticed an e-mail from my grandfather. I opened it up and began to read.

Dear Nicky,

     I always knew you would do fine in New Jersey, regardless of what street you lived on! Remember, when one door closes, another door opens.
See you Saturday,
Pop

    Great, another expression!

Welcome to the Franklin Mason Press Guest Young Author Section

Turn this page for stories from our three newest Guest Young Authors, ages 9-12 years old. From thousands of submissions, these stories were selected by a committee for their creativity, originality, and quality.

Franklin Mason Press believes that children should have a paramount role in literature, including publishing and sharing their stories with the world. We hope you enjoy reading them as much as we did. If you would like to submit a story you have written, keep reading after the stories. Enjoy!

And the winners are...

1st Place Guest Young Author

Kelsey DeFrates Age 9
Haviland Avenue School
Audubon, New Jersey

The Red Headed Monster

There's a Red Headed Monster that lives in my house. I don't know how she got there, she must have been quiet as a mouse. But she came in my house and I don't know how to get her out.

Don't get her mad, because she will blow. People say she is cute, but I really know. She gets me in trouble with my Mom and Dad. She does things to make me crazy and things to make me mad.

The Red Headed Monster follows me and asks me to play. I don't know why my Mom and my Dad let her stay.

She says that she loves me and gives me a kiss, but when I turn around, she gives me her fist. She has a temper the color of her red hair and sometimes it even makes me a little scared.

When the Red Headed Monster runs and screams, I wish to myself it was only a dream. If you have a little sister, you know what I mean!

2nd Place Guest Young Author
Ethan Woods   Age 9
Nye Elementary School
Hummelstwon, Pennsylvania

Why Jack Rabbits Have Big Ears

A long time ago, there was a jack rabbit named Jumper. One dry day in Australia, Jumper saw a turtle with a huge shell. Jumper started to pick on him because of the size of his shell. Turtle felt very sad. Jumper said, "Your shell is as big as a turkey. Turtle felt so miserable, that he went to the wise man for help.

So the wise man followed turtle home

to catch Jumper making fun of him. Well, the jack rabbit named Jumper began picking on turtle as soon as he saw him. The wise man, who was hiding, heard Jumper and cast a spell upon him. The spell made his ears bigger to see what it would be like to be different.

And that is why jack rabbits have big ears. The moral of this story is to never tease others if they look different. It's what's on the inside that counts. said, "Yes, I will." The kids were all happy.

3rd Place Guest Young Author
Cassandra Selsor Age 9
Mary Frank Elementary School
Granger, Indiana

The Poor Old Lady of Liger and Her Tiger

There once was a poor old lady of Liger,
who spent all her money on her pet tiger.
Suddenly, the tiger got fat and started to wear
an old ladies hat.
No one knows what happened to the poor old
lady of Liger.
So what did happen to the poor old lady of
Liger?
She was swallowed up by her pet tiger.

He had nothing to eat,
so he gobbled up her feet.
Then he swallowed the rest of that poor old
lady of Liger.
The tiger then ate a kangaroo,
so he was sent off to the zoo.
The zookeeper there was Mr. Thump,
who was really very plump.
So the tiger swallowed him up, too.
So my friend, never spend money on a tiger
because of what happened to that poor old
lady of Liger.
By Miss Shbiger, a girl of the village of Liger,
who knew that poor old lady and, of course
her tiger.

**A special thanks to Edward Lear & my
wonderful teacher, Mrs. Heying.**

Calling all young authors...

Would you like to be a Guest Young Author?

If you are 9-12 years old and would like to be Franklin Mason Press's next Guest Young Author, read the directions, write your story, and send it in! The first, second, and third place winners receive $50.00, $40.00, and $30.00, respectively, a book, an award, and a party where you get to autograph books. Send us a 150-350 word story about something strange, funny or unusual. Your story may be fiction or non-fiction.

Turn the page for more details!

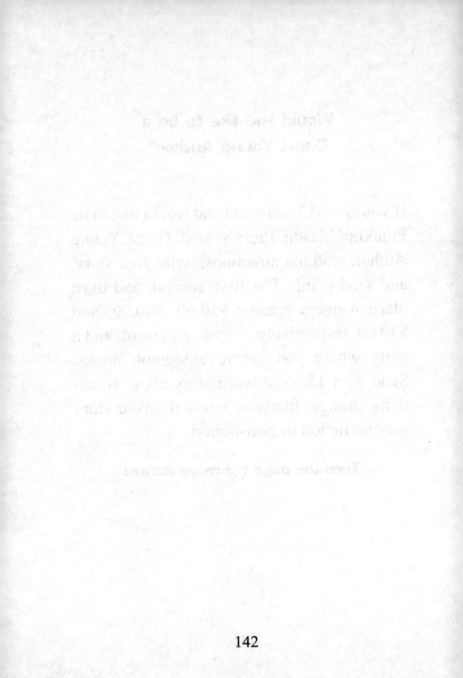

Contest Rules

1. Stories must be typed or handwritten very neatly.

2. Stories containing any violence or inappropriate content will not be considered.

3. Name, age, address, phone number, school, and a parent's signature must be on the back of all submissions.

4. All work must be original and completed solely by the child.

5. Franklin Mason Press reserves the right edit and/or print the submitted material. All work becomes property of Franklin Mason Press and will not be returned. Any work selected will is considered a work-for-hire and Franklin Mason Press reserves all rights.

6. There is no deadline for submissions. All

submissions are considered for the most current title.

7. Only winners will be notified. Once selected, all winners will also be listed on www.franklinmasonpress.com.

Send all submissions to:
    Franklin Mason Press
    Youth Submissions Editor
    PO Box 3808
    Trenton, NJ 08629

Helpful Hints

Write about topics that you know or what you enjoy. If your story is going to be interesting, you need to be interested in your topic.

Use details when describing characters and setting. You want your readers to feel like they've known your characters their whole life and that they have been to your setting

Read your story out loud and really LISTEN to it! If you listen closely, you'll find many things that you would like to change.

Create original characters rather than writing about your favorite cartoon superhero. Keep an idea notebook and whenever you get a great idea that you don't have time to write about, jot it down. Index cards in an index card box (or even a shoe box) are great places to keep ideas safe and handy.

When looking for spelling mistakes, don't trust your eyes or computers, read each line backwards, like the editors do!

Many children's magazines and websites publish children's work, so always be on the look out for places to submit your stories.

When you submit a story, always, always, always follow the directions. Each magazine, publisher, or website will have their own rules and it is important that you follow them.

If your school or local library has a writing club or offers workshops, join in. These are great places to share your work and get new ideas. If your school or library doesn't have one, start one!

After you submit your story, don't wait by the mailbox, start your next story and after that, start your next story, and after that...well, you get the picture.

And, of course, enjoy writing!

About the Author,
Lisa Funari Willever

Lisa Funari Willever wanted to be an author since she was in the third grade and often says if there was a Guest Young Author contest when she was a child, she would have submitted a story a day. *Maybe two a day on weekends!*

She has been a wedding-dress-seller, a file clerk, a sock counter *(really)*, a hostess, waitress, teacher, and author.   While she loved teaching in Trenton, New Jersey, becoming an author has been one of the most exciting adventures of her life. She is a full-time mom and a *night-time author* who travels all over the world visiting schools. She has been to hundreds of schools in dozens of states, including California, South Dakota, Iowa, South Carolina, North Carolina, Florida, Delaware, Connecticut, New York, Pennsylvania, West Virginia, Ohio, Nevada, Idaho, Utah, Alabama, Louisiana, and even the US Navy base in Sasebo, Japan.

Lisa has written several books for children and even a book for new teachers. Her critically acclaimed *Chumpkin* was selected as a favorite by First Lady Laura Bush and displayed at the White House, *Everybody Moos At Cows* was featured on the Rosie O'Donnell Show, and *Garden State Adventure* and *32 Dandelion Court* have been on the prestigious New Jersey Battle of the Books List. Her other titles include *You Can't Walk A Fish, The Easter Chicken, Maximilian The Great, Where Do Snowmen Go?, The Culprit Was A Fly, Miracle on Theodore's Street, Exciting Writing,* and *On Your Mark, Get Set, Teach. Nicky Fifth For Hire* is her thirteenth book and she is currently working on three new titles!

Lisa is married to Todd Willever, a Captain in the Trenton Fire Department. They have three children, Jessica, 8 years old, Patrick, 7 years old, and Timothy Todd, 1 year old. They are also preparing to adopt a little girl from Guatemala (*details in the next book!*).

Lisa was a lifelong resident of Trenton and while she is proud to now reside in the beautiful Mansfield Township, she treasures her 34 years in the city. She is a graduate of

Trenton State College and loves nothing more than traveling with her family and finding creative ways to avoid cooking!

About the Sunshine Foundation

Franklin Mason Press is very proud to donate a portion of each book sale to different children's charities. Like our picture book, *Where Do Snowmen Go?* and the first two Nicky Fifth books, *32 Dandelion Court* and *Garden State Adventure*, *Nicky Fifth For Hire* will benefit The Sunshine Foundation.

In case you aren't familiar with this magnificent and giving group of people, we'd love to tell you about them! The Sunshine Foundation was started by Philadelphia police officer, William Sample who grew to care about many of the patients he protected at St. Christopher's Hospital in Philadelphia. He wished he could grant their wishes and over 20 years later, he and the foundation have granted over 26,500 wishes for children 3 to 21 with diseases and disabilities. They even have a Dream Village in Florida! If you would like to know more, or even better, help them out, you can find them at:

www.sunshinefoundation.org

Nicky Fifth's
Newest Adventure

Nicky Fifth's popularity, both in and out of the state of New Jersey, has been overwhelming! We receive e-mails from families telling us that they are taking their families on Nicky's Garden State day trips!

As a result of the demand and author, Lisa Funari Willever's life-long love for the great Garden State of New Jersey, Nicky's newest adventure is called:

Nicky Fifth's Passport to the Garden State!

Follow Nicky and T-Bone as they become New Jersey's Unofficial Junior Ambassadors. This book includes a passport that may be stamped at various destinations throughout the state, an interactive website, and a scavenger hunt. Now, your family can enjoy the same Garden State Adventures you have been reading about.

Visit www.franklinmasonpress.com for more information.

Nicky Needs You!

Do you have ideas for Nicky's adventures?

Do you live in the Garden State and know about a great place in New Jersey that not too many other people know about?

Send us an e-mail and tell us all about it! Maybe your idea will end up in the next Nicky Fifth book!

www.nickyfifth.com

To celebrate Nicky Fifth's 5th Anniversary, take the Nicky Fifth Quiz!

1. What are Nicky's parents' names?

2. Why is he called Nicky Fifth?

3. Who is Nicky's best friend in Philly?

4. Name Nicky's teacher in Philadelphia.

5. What is Nicky's New Jersey address?

6. Name Nicky's brother and sisters.

7. How does Nicky feel about moving?

8. What is Nicky's mom's favorite holiday?

9. What is Nicky's dad's job?

10. Who always uses expressions when talking to Nicky?

(turn the page for the answers)

Nicky Fifth Quiz Answers

1. Jim and Erin

2. He lived on Fifth Street

3. Joey Grapes

4. Mrs. Bailey

5. 32 Dandelion Court (of course!)

6. Timmy, Maggie, and Emma

7. Absolutely miserable

8. St. Patrick's Day

9. Produce manager

10. His grandfather